A Baker's Dozen

Erie Canal Adventures
BOOK II

by Lettie A. Petrie
Illustrated by Beth Petrie

Additional Titles By Author

Adirondack Fairy Tales
1997

Tell Me a Story
Adirondack Fairy Tales II
2002

Minnie the Mule and the Erie Canal
Erie Canal Series Book I
2001

A Baker's Dozen
Erie Canal Adventures
Book II

by Lettie A. Petrie
Copyright ©2003

Illustrated by Beth L. Petrie
Westdale, New York 13483

Printed in the United States of America
by Patterson Press, Michigan

Library of Congress Cataloguing-in-Publication Data

CIP applied for

ISBN 0-9711638-2-0

Published By

PETRIE PRESS
9 Card Avenue
Camden, NY 13316

A Baker's Dozen

Erie Canal Adventures – Book II

by Lettie A. Petrie
Illustrated by Beth Petrie

DEDICATION

*This book is dedicated with love
to all of my children and grandchildren
as well as our new generation
of great grandchildren....Because history and
our heritage are important to all of us.*

ALL ABOUT
A Baker's Dozen: Erie Canal Adventures – Book II

You are about to enter the year of 1850 in what was once the "wilderness" village of Rome, New York. Rome is rapidly approaching the time it will become a city, partly because of the Erie Canal which brought the world to its shores.

Twenty-five years ago the canal opened farther south in the village than its citizens wanted it to be.[1] New legislation made it possible to divert the path of the canal to a short distance from Dominick Street, the hub of its business district, before this story took place.[2] It was an exciting time to live in Rome.

Local business people had their stores all along Dominick Street, west and east of the American Corner where James Street crossed. At this point the village was referred to as West Rome or East Rome. While there were no paved roads, coal-gas lamps that were lighted each night by the village lamplighter illuminated the streets.[3]

The Erie Canal, visible from Dominick Street, was busy with traffic going east to New York City's harbor and west to Buffalo. It was intersected in east Rome by the recently completed Black River Canal, going North to the Adirondacks.

This canal provided a way to float lumber from the north to be added to cargo on the Erie. Trains now ran from Rome, west, all the way to Buffalo[4] as well as to the east and New York City, often following the path of the Erie Canal.

You are about to meet the Gleasons who have just come west on the canal from Amsterdam to take possession of their new farm. And so their story begins….

TRUE FACTS

1. The canal first opened south of the village, crossing near South James Street.
2. When the canal was moved it ran along the same path that is now Erie Boulevard.
3. Gas lights were installed in Rome in 1851.
4. The train route was expanded to reach Buffalo in 1850.

Contents

Chapter ONE

A New Beginning

Captain John Fairweather's barge docked at the village of Rome's marina. His brother, Dan, partner in the freight business they shared on the busy Erie Canal, heaved the landing ramp over the side of their barge to the tow path below.

First down the sloping ramp were Captain John's daughter, Sarah, and her new friend, Abby Gleason, both thirteen. The two girls nimbly jumped the last few feet before they turned to meet Sarah's cousin, Jack, who led Minnie, her favorite of her father's mules, down to the tow path from the barge's bow stable.

They were joined quickly by Abby's brother, Andy, a year older than his sister. "So, this is Rome!" He grinned as he looked up at the rise of the wide dirt road.

"You bet! It is a great place to live." Jack was enthusiastic. "I sort of wish it was our last trip for the season so we could be the ones to show you around the village. I'm glad we will be here for a few days while Pa and Uncle John get the next load on board, and see you settled."

They turned as Abby and Andy's parents came down the ramp. Rose Gleason was much more cautious than her children. She lifted her long skirt, stepped carefully, and held firmly to her husband's shoulder as he walked down before her.

Jack finished fastening the big barge to one of the iron spikes embedded in the Canal's side and prepared to lead Minnie away from the edge. She nodded approvingly. *Good! I always remember that time I got pushed into the canal by that nasty Mike! It pays to be careful.* She snorted as she followed him to the road.

Sarah's parents, Abigail and John Fairweather, joined them on the towpath with his brother Dan and his wife, Mabel. "We made good time! You will have all day to unpack and get settled." The Captain grinned at Rose and Michael Gleason. "You have inherited a fine big farm. Your Uncle Andrew was well liked. I hope you are going to be happy here."

"It was a piece of luck for me that we could arrange for you to make this special trip from Amsterdam with me and my family, and all of our belongings. When Neil Anderson said you were making a second trip in that direction this year, and put me in touch with you when you pastured your mules with him in Watervliet, we were grateful. It sure beats coming by train or wagon." Michael smiled at his new friends.

Jack grinned. "Sarah always likes stopping at Watervliet. It gives her a chance to see her boyfriend, Teddy Anderson."

Sarah stuck her tongue out at him. Her cheeks were pink as she retorted, "You just wish you had a girl-friend!"

Abby knew all about how Jack liked to tease Sarah, and she changed the subject. "Can we hurry up and get unloaded? I can't wait to see our new house!" Her freckled face was eager, and her curly red hair bounced on her shoulders as she jumped up and down.

"Calm down, Abby. It will be a while before we are

ready to go." Her mother chided her, but she knew just how she was feeling.

"Jack, run up to Mr. Smith's livery stable and tell him we are ready for his flatbed wagon. I told him we would be coming in today." His father took Minnie's reins.

"Can Andy come with me?"

"Can I, Pa?" Andy, who was as freckled as his sister, and had curly red hair too, looked at his father eagerly.

"I don't see why not." Michael stretched his six-foot frame and stamped the tow path. "I am glad to reach dry land! I would never make a sailor."

"Well, we will be glad to have a blacksmith in town, I can tell you! And a place to board the mules when we are here. I was more than willing to haul you and your family. Let's get as much as we can down on the path before they get back."

He was watching the two long-legged boys head up the long rise towards Dominick Street, just a short distance from them. It was Rome's main street, the center of the business district. The citizens of Rome had been unhappy when the Erie Canal was opened in 1825, near the southern edge of the village. It took a few years for them to convince the legislature of the state that it would be to their advantage to divert the canal and move it closer to the village business section. Farmers, mostly of Italian descent, settled near the fertile muck lands that had partially resulted from the move, and their crops thrived. People in the village found they liked the advantage of being close to the canal traffic.

"We can help with some of the lighter things." Abigail lifted her long skirt and followed the men up the ramp, and Mabel and Rose followed close behind her.

Abby and Sarah stood together, stroking Minnie's soft muzzle. She lowered her big head and gently nudged them. *It is good to be home! No walking for a few days!*

"I didn't know if I wanted to leave Amsterdam. All of my friends are there," Abby confessed. "Do you think I will make any friends here this summer.... before school starts?" She shook her head ruefully. "This was all so sudden. Mama and Papa told Uncle Andrew they would take good care of his farm some day, but we were all really sad when he got sick and died so suddenly while he was visiting us."

"Your farm is really close to downtown, and there are a lot of girls our age here in Rome." Sarah giggled as she added, "and boys too! You will meet some of them this summer, and you may forget all about me before we get back for good this year."

"No I won't! We are going to be best friends. Remember, you promised!"

"I know. Usually I would hate to come home when it is time for school, but I will be happy this summer because I will see you again." Sarah hugged her new friend.

By the time that most of their belongings were piled on the dock, the boys came back, riding on the empty flatbed wagon that Mr. Smith drove briskly down the road. Captain John introduced him to Michael and his family and the old man shook hands firmly. "I'll be glad to have a blacksmith so handy.... and someone to take some of the boarding load off my shoulders. Rome is growing so fast that my stable can't take care of all the traffic."

"That is good to hear! I worried about uprooting my family and coming so far. You don't mind the added stable in town?" Michael was relieved.

"No. There is talk that the village may incorporate

with the Town of Rome and become a city before too many years pass. I'll tell you, with the canal business and the railroads growing like they are, this is a village that is busting at the seams."

B·PETRIE

Chapter TWO

Coming Home

"It is beautiful! Just look, Mama!" Abby clasped her hands in awe. She was standing in the drive leading to the big white farm house that was to become their new home. Back in Amsterdam, they had lived in one of a row of small houses, and her father had his blacksmith shop in the city.

"It is so pretty!" Her mother hugged her, almost as excited as her daughter.

"Beauty is not what we are looking for – it's a home that we want." Michael laughed as he grabbed his wife's hand and hurried down the drive to where five wide steps led to a porch that spread across the front of the house, and wrapped around its sides. A center door was flanked on either side by two tall windows with dark blue shutters. He could feel his heart pounding with excitement. "Come on, Andy!"

"I'm right behind you, Pa." Andy struggled to pull one of the big trunks off the flatbed wagon.

"Leave those until we see what is inside." They stood together, gazing at the house. It stood in the shade of a circle of big maple trees, heavy with summer foliage. "We will want to see the outbuildings before we unload too." They moved up the steps that led to the front door. White pillars rose to support the porch roof, just below the second floor's row of windows, and the dormer windows above that were a part of the third floor.

Abby rushed ahead to grasp the knob of the wide door.

"Not so fast! I have the key." Her father laughed as he reached into his pocket. "Remember that lawyer fellow who met us while we were loading the wagon?"

"Hurry, Papa! I can't wait to see it!" The door swung in and Abby was first to enter. Doors lined either side of the wide hall, and at the far end they could see another open door facing them.

"Look, I will bet this is the company parlor!" Abby peeked into the first room on her left, and then rushed in. Two love seats, padded in dark green tapestry, sat on either side of a brick fireplace. A brown carpet covered part of the wide, planked floor, and small tables and chairs were scattered around the big room. Two windows faced the porch they had just crossed, and white curtains, dingy with age, limply covered their dusty panes. There was a faint musty odor.

"This house needs us! It has been closed up too long." Rose turned slowly, taking in the big room, as her nose wrinkled at the smell. She went and threw up one of the windows.

"There is another room over here." Andy had gone to the other side of the hall, and they joined him in the room across from them. A big roll-topped desk sat between the two front windows, with a leather covered chair facing it. Matching leather chairs were beside tables that held books on their surface, and the back wall was entirely covered by shelves full of books. The wooden floor was bare, and the windows had no curtains.

"I will bet this is where Uncle Andrew spent most

of his time after Aunt Lucy died. It is probably where he did his books." Michael looked sad as he gazed around the library. "He must have been lonely in this big house after she was gone."

"Let's go and see my kitchen. Uncle Andrew told me he knew I would like it." Rose took her husband's hand and led him down the hall, past two more rooms – a dining room, and a smaller sitting room – into a kitchen that made her gasp. It stretched the width of the house, and had a huge fireplace on the back wall. There was a beehive oven[1] at one side, and an opening with a cooking spit took the rest of the hearth. On the knotty pine wall nearest the hall a big black range sat, dusty from disuse. Cupboards filled every wall space, and a long trestle table stretched down the entire middle of the room. A wooden dry-sink sat next to a metal sink with a pump, near a door leading to a back porch at the far end. The planked floor was almost white from what must have been frequent scrubbing.

Rose wiped her misty eyes with the back of one hand as she looked around her. "It is like a dream come true! I have always dreamed of having a kitchen like this!" She ran a hand over the surface of the cooking range. "I cannot wait to try a roast in this oven….and a pie and bread in that beehive oven over there. Uncle Andrew told me about the things Lucy made. He said she loved to cook, and he made this kitchen for her."

"Look, Pa, there are stairs over here. Let's go up and see what is there at the top." Andy had opened a door at the far end, near the door to the side porch.

They all climbed a steep flight of stairs that opened onto a wide hallway with two doors on each side. There were four bedrooms, each with a wide bed covered with a patchwork quilt. Beside each bed a braided rug waited to warm cold toes from the wooden floor. Two front bedrooms had windows with wide window seats. The two back bedrooms were even bigger, and they were full of dressers and wardrobes that Michael's uncle had crafted.

Andy, always impatient to see everything, pulled a long cord hanging at the back end of the hall, and jumped back when part of the ceiling dropped to disclose a trapdoor leading to yet another floor. When Michael pulled another cord, a flight of narrow stairs unfolded, and they climbed them to enter a huge loft that spread across the entire house.

Abby peeked around her father and gazed at the big room. Sunlight filtered through dusty dormer windows on both front and back walls. "What a great place to play!"

"Michael, I cannot believe that this is all ours." Rose came to stand near him.

"It is though." He put his arm around her shoulders. She was much smaller than him. Her red hair barely reached his shoulder, and her green eyes shone with happiness as she looked around the loft. Michael added softly, "Uncle Andrew and Aunt Lucy always hoped for a big family, and they never had children. They lived for each other and their neighbors. When she died he just lost his desire to live, I think. Remember, he was so lonely that he left here last winter to visit us, and he told us that when he was gone this would all be ours? I never dreamed that influenza would take him so quickly."

Rose nodded. "He said that his stay with us was the best thing that happened to him after Lucy was gone." She pressed her cheek against his arm, and laughed softly. "He wanted us to be happy here. He said maybe we would fill these rooms with children."

Michael chuckled. "We have a good start. If that is what the good Lord means us to do, so be it."

"Look, Pa. Here comes the other wagons with more of our stuff." Andy pushed up a front window, and leaned out. They clattered down the stairs to meet the new arrivals. Michael and Andy went with Captain John, Dan and Jack to help Mr. Smith unload the tools Michael would need for his blacksmith shop out in the barn, and the women and girls went inside. Jack and Andy led the three mules into the stable where six stalls stood waiting, and Minnie whinnied her approval. *Now this is going to make a nice place to spend the winter months!* Her sister mules agreed as they looked around the big barn.

Mr. Smith looked around with more than a little envy. "Your uncle sure had a knack for organizing things. It looks like you could start your business today!"

"Look Pa! There's a little house out here in back. I wonder what it is for?" Andy had gone to the back door at the far end of the barn and Michael followed him outside to where they saw a small building with a slanted roof standing to the right, near a kitchen garden. "Uncle Andrew told me about this. He said that he and Aunt Lucy lived there while he was building the big house. He always kept it in good repair for visitors."

He walked over to the left, where another small building proved to be a chicken coop with an added stall at its end. "This must be the hen house and cow barn he built for Lucy to keep her milk cow and chickens." He laughed. "He said he built it so she could have an unlimited supply of eggs and milk for her cooking."

"You will have to make it bigger for Mama, probably."

Andy grinned. "She isn't happy if she doesn't have her hands in flour."

"You are right." His father put his arm around his son's shoulders as they explored the land around their farm with the other men. Before they went inside, they found the storerooms his uncle had told him about, and the ice house where they would keep their food cold. It stood next to the stone smokehouse that would hold their supplies of meat.

"If I didn't love the life we lead on the canal, I could be mighty happy on a place like this." John Fairweather clapped his new friend on the shoulder as they finished unloading the barn supplies and went in to enjoy the dinner Rose and the others had prepared. They sat down at the long trestle table to eat their first meal in their new home with their friends around them.

Michael bowed his head as they were seated. "We thank you for your many blessings, Lord and we promise we will give back to our neighbors and friends some of the good things you have seen fit to give us."

"Amen." His wife smiled through her tears as she looked around the table. "I hope that Uncle Andrew knows what joy he has given us."

1. Beehive ovens built into the bricks of the fireplace and heated with coals from the bed of the fireplace were used widely to bake in colonial America.

Chapter THREE

The Family Grows

Rose moved quickly around her kitchen, singing softly to herself as she laid out her baking supplies on the long kitchen table.

"Oh drat! I'm out of sugar!" She went to the back stairs and called, "Abby, will you come down? I need to have you go up to the market."

Abby laid aside the book she had been reading as she sat curled on the window seat of her bedroom. She had chosen this room because she loved sitting there, dreaming about her plans for going to her new school in just a few more weeks. *I can hardly wait to see Sarah again. She has only been back once since we moved here, and then only for three days while her father reloaded his barge, but she took me to visit Kitty while she was here. I like Kitty. We will all be in the same grade when I start school.*

"Abby, are you coming? Did you hear me?" Her mother called again, and she reluctantly started down the back stairway.

"I'm here." She entered the kitchen, sniffing the delicious aroma of an apple pie cooling on the table.

"I need to have you go up to the market and pick up some sugar for me." Rose smiled at her daughter. "I thought you might like to stop at Kitty's house and

take this pie in to her family. Tell her I will be stopping there this afternoon to give her mother a hand with the little ones." Rose was concerned about how ill Kitty's mother had been when she stopped there two days ago. She had met the family in church, and they became friends. In the two months that the Gleason family had lived in Rome quite a few people had come to visit after bringing their horses to be shod out in Michael's blacksmith shop. She could hear the distant ring of his hammer through the kitchen's open door now. Andy was out there, helping his father. This was a bigger stable than Michael had ever had before, and he and Andy were working long hours to get the neglected grounds back in shape.

"Can I ask Kitty to come and visit this afternoon? She could bring the twins with her and Susey, and her mother could rest."

Her mother smiled. "I guess that would be all right. Have you done all of your chores? Are the bedrooms tidy?"

Abby nodded. "I finished them a long time ago. I have been reading up in my room."

"Take this money and try not to stay too long. I want to get my baking done before the heat of the day."

Abby walked down the wide, dusty road, admiring the leafy maple trees lining the lane. She turned, as she neared the village at the corner of James Street and walked up to Dominick Street where most of the shops were. Kitty and her family lived in a small frame house they rented on East Dominick Street. Her father had been killed two years ago in a lumber camp accident, just before her little sister, Susey was born. Abby sighed, thinking how lucky she was that her family was all together. Kitty's mother took in washing and sewed for other people to support herself and her four children. Rose had sent her some of Abby's outgrown things to cut down for six-year-old Meggie, one of the twins, and she sent them bread and other things from her kitchen as often as she could. The apple pie Abby was taking to her now should be a real treat for them.

The front door of the tiny house was open. Meggie and her twin, Joey, were sitting on the small stoop with Susey between them and they were all crying.

"What is wrong?" Abby put her basket down and picked the crying baby up. "Where is Kitty? Is your mother still sick?"

"The doctor is in there." Joey jerked a thumb at the door. "He told us to come out here."

Kitty appeared in the doorway, her eyes red and swollen. When she saw Abby, she burst into tears. "Abby! Can you get your mama and come back? Doctor Bill says we need help." She gulped her tears back, wiping her eyes with the back of her hand. "Meggie, you and Joey take Susey next door to Mrs. Kelly's and ask if you can stay with her for a little while. I have to go back inside." She watched her sisters and brother until they obediently started for the house next to theirs.

"What is wrong, Kitty? Can I do anything? I just brought you this pie." Abby held out the basket. "I will go right back and get Mama, but what should I tell her? Is your mama worse?"

Tears poured down Kitty's pale cheeks. "Doctor Bill says she is dying." Her voice was just a whisper. "He says we need a grown-up here to help us."

"I will be back right away." Abby hugged her friend and then ran back the way she had come, as fast as she could go. She burst through the back door, and when Rose saw her flushed face, she dropped her mixing spoon back in the bowl and put her arms around her.

"What is wrong, honey? Did you lose your money? Or did you drop the pie? Don't cry, everyone has accidents once in a while." She smoothed Abby's curly hair back from her forehead.

"Mama! Kitty says her mother is dying! The doctor says they need a grown-up to help. Kitty wants to know if you can come!"

"Oh, my Lord! Of course I will come. Let's just take a minute to tell your father, and then we will go." She took off her apron as she spoke, and she quickly checked her ovens and pots before she went out to the barn with Abby.

Michael was paring the hoof of a spirited young mare. He was sitting with her foot folded back onto his black leather apron when he looked up and saw them. Andy was just behind him, sweeping the aisle of the barn floor.

"Hey! Did you bring us a treat?" Andy grinned as he saw them coming.

Michael, seeing Abby's flushed face, and his wife's worried look, carefully placed the horse's hoof on the ground and stood up. "Something is wrong?"

Quickly, Rose told him that she was going with Abby to see how they could help Kitty's family. He nodded. "You take all the time that you need. I will come along too as soon as I finish up here."

When they reached the house, Rose went inside without knocking. She had been here several times in the past few days, so she was prepared for the scantily furnished little place. Kate Scanlon's house was usually spic-and-span, but today clothes were everywhere, and she could smell the unwashed diapers thrown on the floor under the kitchen table. Above all of the other odors was the distinctive smell that she knew from experience was present when death draws near. Kitty was sitting in a chair next to the table with her arms wrapped around her waist, and her blue eyes were swimming in tears. She was Abby's age, but much smaller, so thin that Rose could feel her bones as she put her arms around her.

She looked up as Doctor Bill Andrews came out of the bedroom just off the kitchen, and she saw his look of relief when he saw her. She knew he had bad news. "Why don't you two girls go outside and sit in the sun while the doctor and I talk?"

Kitty jumped up quickly. "Yes! Let's go outside, Abby."

Abby looked fearfully at her mother, but she went with her friend as Rose turned back to the doctor.

She had met him and his wife at church a few weeks before. "How bad is it?"

"She has only a few minutes left, I am afraid. She has been hanging on to talk to you, I think. Are you up to it?" He looked at her pale face with compassion.

Rose took a deep breath. "Yes. We cared for Michael's uncle during his sickness with influenza a few months ago. That is what Kate has, isn't it?"

He nodded. "Yes. If you could just comfort her – reassure her about her children." He sighed. "God only knows what will become of them. They have no family. Right now, I just want to make her last minutes as easy as we can. When she is gone we will do whatever we have to."

Rose went down on her knees next to the bed and

took Kate's cold hand in hers. "I am here, Kate." Her voice was soft, and her friend smiled weakly when she opened her eyes.

"I knew you would come if I asked. Rose, promise me you will take care of my children! Don't let them put them in the County Poor House or the orphanage. Please? Please keep them together. They will have no one now."

Rose felt a tremor go through her whole body. *Four children! How can I care for four more children?* She drew a deep breath, and somehow found the strength to smile at her friend. "You rest easy, Kate your children will be just fine."

Kate's hand gripped hers with all of her waning strength. "Promise me? Please!"

"We promise you, Kate. Rose and I will take your children." It was Michael who answered. He had come in as she heard Kate's plea. Now he reached down and squeezed his wife's shoulder firmly.

And Kate smiled for the last time before she closed her eyes.

While the doctor took care of the arrangements for Kate, Rose and her husband gathered up the weeping children and took them home with them.

The twins were bewildered, and two-year-old Susey clung tightly to Rose, wrapping her arms around her neck every time she started to put her down. Kitty appeared dazed. Rose looked up at her tall, dark-haired husband as he strode along the road with her. He had stooped to pick Joey up and the little boy put his dark head down on his shoulder with a sigh of relief. Andy picked Meggie up when she fell, and they all walked the rest of the way in silence.

When they reached the house, they went in the

back door to the kitchen, and Michael placed his burden in one of the chairs. Andy sat Meggie next to the little boy.

"Andy, up in the loft you will find your sister's old highchair. I think we will need it down here now." His father's voice was quiet. He stroked Joey's hair back, and ran his fingers through Meggie's dark curls. "Abby, why don't you and Kitty go in the pantry and get us some bread for sandwiches and we will have some lunch. We need to talk." He reached for the little girl who clung to Rose's neck, and cradled her in his arms as he sat at the head of the table.

Rose knew what he was doing. She had faith that he would know how to reassure these children, but she thought again, *what are we going to do with four more children?*

Michael chuckled softly. "It seems that Uncle Andrew was right." He smiled at her as she moved to bring food to the table. "This house was meant to be full of children."

She rolled her eyes at him, but she had to laugh. "Do you think he knew it would be four at a time?"

Andy brought the wooden high chair from the loft and sat it at the end of the table. Susey settled into it without protest when Rose handed her a piece of fresh bread, spread with jelly. They all sat around the table, and Michael looked at his own two children. "This is something that we all need to talk about. If Kitty and her brother and sisters want to stay with us, would that upset you? Would you be willing to share with them and let them join our family?"

"Oh, yes! Kitty can be my sister!" Abby was eager.

"I could let Joey share my room." Andy offered.

"What about Susey and Meggie?" Kitty looked

dazed. "Will you really let all of us stay here?"

Rose chuckled. "It appears that we would. It is a good thing we have a big house. We will have to bring our old crib down from the loft for Susey. Meggie can sleep with you, Kitty, in the room next to Abby, and we will put Susey's crib next to your bed. How does that sound?"

"My mama is not coming back….is she?" Joey's lips quivered, and tears slipped down his cheeks.

Rose went to put her arms around him. "I promised your mama that you children can always stay with us, and that made her happy. She was very sick, Joey, but now she is in a beautiful place, and she will be well again." Rose hugged him to her as she sat next to him.

"We are all going to be sad when we think of your mama leaving us, and we will miss her, but after a while we will all be happy again. I promise you." Michael looked around at the trusting faces that were turned to him.

Slowly they looked at each other, and then nodded solemnly as they took a bite of the sandwiches they had been given.

Chapter FOUR

Back to School!

"Hurry now." Rose finished buttoning Susey's dress. She sat her on the edge of the table to button her shoes, but her eyes were on the row of eager faces across from her. It was the first day of school.

"We are in the very first classes to go to the new school on Liberty Street!"[1] Abby spun around making her new plaid dress swirl around her legs.

"Jack and I took a walk up there yesterday." Andy was brushing his unruly red curls before the mirror over the kitchen sink. "It is really something! Every grade has a separate room this year! And the building has two floors! I guess Jack and I will be upper class-men. Jack was glad that he and Sarah got back in time for the first day."

"I am happy that the school is not too far for all of you to walk. It was so nice that Captain Fairweather's family got back. Abigail and Mabel will stay home now while their husbands finish out the season on the canal."

Rose smiled as she surveyed the line of children eagerly waiting to leave. She put Susey on the floor and went around the table to smooth Andy's hair off his forehead, brush Joey's hair back, and tighten Meggie's ribbons. She smiled approvingly at Kitty and Abby's shining faces. "Come out to the barn with me.

Your father is going to watch Susey for me while I walk up to see you started this morning."

Michael looked up with a grin as his wife and her brood of children entered the blacksmith shop in the front part of the stable. "All set?"

"Yes. You are sure you can watch Susey while I am gone? I would not have asked you to except that it is really too far to carry her. She is getting to be a big girl." Rose looked at the iron that Michael was working on. "You are not too busy to take care of her?"

"No problem. See, I finished the pen I told you I was making for her." He took Susey into his arms and walked a few steps to a small pen with wooden spindles, bending to place her in its middle. She promptly stood up to grasp the top rail in her chubby hands and chortled in delight at the beads he had strung between the spindles. "Look at the blocks that I made for you, Pumpkin." He leaned over to show her a pile of small wooden blocks, and Susey sank down on her bottom to take some of them into her lap. He smiled at his wife. "See, no way she can get hurt in there. When you get back I'll take it into the kitchen for you. It will make it easy to keep track of her while the children are in school."

"What would I do without you!" His wife reached up to kiss his tanned cheek. "How do we look? Do you think your children will make you proud?"

Michael grinned as he looked at the five eager faces. "You will certainly do that. Have all of you got your books and your lunches?"

"You bet!" Andy's grin matched his father's. "But, if we don't get started, we will be late."

Rose held Meggie and Joey's hands as they walked down the lane until they reached James Street and turned to go up the hill to Dominick Street. "Does any-one know why this is called the 'Busy Corner'?" They paused at the intersection.

"I do." Andy slowed his steps. "Dominick Lynch[2] founded this village way back when he came to this part of the country and bought a big piece of land. He owned most of Rome back then, only he called it Lynchville. It was changed to Rome later."

"What has that got to do with this being the Busy Corner?" Abby said. "You think you are so smart Andy."

"Wait a minute! He made a map of how this village would look, and he named some of the streets after his family. This street we just came up is James Street, after one of his sons, and Dominick Street, where we cross, he named after himself. He planned it to be the main street and center of the village, with most of the stores and businesses all along here….so that is why it is called the busy corner. Some people call it the "American Corner", because no matter where they come from the shop owners are Americans now."

"How did you learn about that, Andy?" Rose was always surprised that he was so quick to find out about his surroundings.

"Mr. Rowley,[3] over at the Rome Sentinel newspaper told me. He started to run the paper this year, but he says he has worked there since he was about eleven-years-old, and he knows all about how Rome has been growing. He says I can work for him if you and Pa let me. Can I, Mama?"

"I don't know, Andy. Your father needs you to help him. We will have to talk to him about it."

"Well, I hope you decide that I can. We could use the money. I heard you and Papa talking about how much it will cost for all of us to go to this new public school because it is going to be supported by the taxes everyone will have to pay." Andy pointed at the big building on the corner just across from them as they crossed and continued up the next block. "Mr. Rowley said that this whole area was rebuilt after the big fire[4] of 1846 destroyed so many buildings. That is when the Rome Sentinel moved over there where it is now."

"Come on! We are going to be late." Abby and Kitty, two steps ahead of them, turned to urge them on. Liberty Street, the next crossing, was where they turned left and walked another block to the new brick building where they would go to school. It had been finished just this summer.

Sarah and Jack were waiting at the front door for them. "I thought you would never get here!" Sarah's freckled face reflected her excitement.

"Yeah! Come on, Andy. You and I are in the same room." Jack opened the door.

"Can we go ahead?" Andy turned to his mother. "Remember, we registered last week, and you know where our room is."

"Yes. You boys can go ahead. Kitty and Abby, you can go to your room with Sarah too. I will take Meggie and Joey to meet their teacher. Remember now, you are to wait for them after school and bring them home with you."

"We will!" They turned to walk rapidly down the wide hallway. Rose shook her head in amusement. *They are always in a rush!* Meggie and Joey clung to her hands as she took them into their classroom to meet their new teacher. This would be their first year in school. Rose smiled as she introduced them to their teacher. *She looks so young! I will bet she is just out of Normal School herself.*

Miss Walker looked down at her list. "I see that these are foster children. Does that mean that they may not stay long?"

"No. They are part of our family now and they will be staying with us always." Rose's voice was firm.

"We are staying with Aunt Rose and Uncle Michael forever!" Joey clutched Rose's hand tightly. "Aren't we, Meggie?"

"Yes!" Meggie nodded vehemently.

Rose smiled at them. *We have come a long way in the weeks they have been with us. It has been a while since any of them have had nightmares, or come to crawl in with Michael and me during the night.* "Their older brother and sisters will come for them when school lets out. If you have any problems please let me know."

She hurried back the way she had come, and looked with pleasure at the business district. It stretched on both sides of the Busy Corner, and some of the markets and restaurants were finding room on side streets too. It was easy to see that this was a good place to start a new business. *I am glad the village is still growing. It should make it easier for us now that our family is so big. Just the cost of keeping the children in school is going to take a big part of our income. Well, there is no use in fretting. God will provide if we work hard.* She refused to waste her time worrying on this beautiful day.

As she neared the farm's driveway she noticed how quiet it was. There was no ring of hammer against metal. She hurried down the drive, and went directly to the barn.

Michael stood in the doorway, talking with a man and woman and a small boy. As she grew closer, she hesitated. *They are Negroes!* She had seen people of color in Amsterdam once or twice, but from what she had heard, most of them lived in the South. They were the property of wealthy plantation owners, and rumor had it that there were a lot of problems developing across the country about people owning slaves. *I wonder how they came to be here? Are they waiting for their owners to come and pick them up?*

Michael saw her coming and smiled. "I told you that I was expecting my wife back, and here she is."

As she came closer, Rose saw that the woman was holding Susey in her arms, and the little girl reached her arms out to Rose.

"Mama!" Susey had started to call her that after a few weeks with the family, and Rose loved her dearly. She hugged her soft little body as she took her into her arms.

"Rose, this is Ben Williams and his wife, Esther." Michael patted the tight curls on the little boy's head who stood next to him. "And this is Eli."

"I am pleased to meet you." Rose tried not to look surprised. If these people were slaves, she had no idea why they would be here at their farm.

"Ben and his family came up the canal from Albany with a canawler and his barge. Ben worked for him on the way. It seems that he met Captain Fairweather and John told him about us and about our farm. They are hoping we might have some work for them." Michael kept his face expressionless with an effort. He was wondering just how to handle this, and he had no idea how Rose would react.

"Work for us? But Michael...." Her voice trailed off. *How do I ask them if they are runaway slaves?*

The man Michael called Ben smiled. He seemed to

sense her confusion. His teeth were a startling white against his dark skin. "We are free people, Miz Gleason. We made our way up North so we could stay free."

"I see." She was bewildered. *They must be hungry if they have just come off the canal. At least I can feed them.* She turned to the woman and the little boy who stood next to her. "Are you hungry? Why don't you come inside and I'll put on a pot of coffee. Would you like a cookie and some milk?" She smiled at the little boy, whose big brown eyes had remained fastened on her face.

His dark eyes lit up, and he licked his lips. "Yes, Ma'am!"

"Come on then. Michael, can you leave your work? We can talk better inside."

Rose and Esther went first with the two children, and she put Susey into her high chair, watching Esther's admiring glance around her kitchen.

"Goodness! This kitchen must make your work like child's play!" Esther's brown eyes scanned the big room, and she hesitated. "Could I maybe help you set the table?"

Rose realized that she was nervous, and she decided it might be a good thing to let her help. "My dishes are there in the cupboard. If you won't mind setting places for us, I will make the coffee and take care of washing these breakfast plates that I didn't clear away before I took the children to school."

"You have more children? Eli, you sit down quiet there in your chair." Esther hurried over to the cupboard that Rose had pointed to.

"We have five more children." Rose chuckled as she saw Esther's surprised look. "I will have to tell you about them, but right now, I know you must be hungry." She set the coffee pot on the range to heat.

By the time that Michael and Ben came in, carrying Susey's pen between them, the two women were talking like old friends, and the table held a hastily prepared lunch.

It was late in the afternoon when the children came home from school. Abby and Kitty had Meggie between them, holding her hands, and Joey was struggling to keep up with Andy's long strides as he ran along beside him.

As they approached the barn they could see Michael talking to someone, and a small figure came slowly outside as Eli smiled at them shyly.

"There you are! We have exciting news for you! Eli and his mother and father are going to be staying with us. Ben is going to help me out here in the shop and his wife is going to work with Mama in the house. Now that you are all in school, we thought we could use their help."

Andy was the first to come forward. He hesitantly offered his hand to Ben, and was rewarded with a wide grin.

Joey followed quickly. He had imitated anything that Andy did from the day he came to live with them. He looked at Ben and Eli with frank curiosity. "You are black! I never saw nobody with black skin before. Will it wash off?"

Michael chuckled. "Joey's questions are something we all have to get used to, I guess. Ben and his family are negro, Joey. Their skin is a different color than ours. Some people have freckles like Abby and Andy, and some people don't have them. Some people have white skin, and some have dark, like Ben and Eli. Do you understand?"

"I guess so." Joey looked at Eli. They were almost the same size. "Do you want to play after I change my school clothes?"

Eli looked up at his father, and Ben nodded.

"Yes, I would."

"Come on!" Joey started for the house, and then turned back. "Where is Aunt Rose?"

"She is out in the little house in back of the stable, helping Eli's mother get settled."

"Can we go and see?" Abby and Kitty released Meggie's hands, and she ran back to the house with Joey and Eli.

"Are you really going to stay with us? All the time? Are they, Papa?" Abby didn't know how she felt about that. Her family was changing so fast! "Where will everyone sleep?"

"Ben and his family are going to live in our little guest house. We have been bringing some of the furniture out of the loft. Why don't you girls go out and see for yourself."

They could hear Rose laughing as they neared the door of the little cabin. Kitty had not been inside it before. There was a small porch in front, with a sloping roof, and the door they entered took them into a big room with a fireplace on one wall. There were two chairs standing at either side of the stone hearth, and a sofa stood between the chairs. A big braided rug covered the wooden floor. As they walked on tiptoe across to the doorway facing them, Abby's mother came out to greet them. "Here you are! Was your first day of school exciting?"

"Yes! We are both in seventh grade, and there are a lot of other girls there." Kitty's blue eyes twinkled. "A lot of boys too, and I think one of them really likes Abby."

Oh, he does not, Kitty! He was just being polite." Abby's cheeks turned a bright pink.

"Well, he didn't offer to carry *my* books home!"

Rose laughed as she hugged her daughter. "I want you girls to meet Esther. She and her husband and their little boy will be staying with us. We are trying to make them comfortable out here in their own little house."

Esther straightened up as she turned from the cupboard across from them and smiled. "It sounds like you had a real good day in school." She looked closely at them. Kitty was small and blonde, and it was easy to see that Abby was Rose's daughter. She had the same red hair and green eyes as her mother. "I wish Eli could go to school. Ben and I do our best to teach him his reading and writing."

"Why can't he go to school? Isn't he old enough?" Abby asked her.

"We can't go to white folks schools." Esther was embarrassed, and she quickly turned to Rose.

"Wait a minute, Esther! I think we should see if Eli can go to school." Rose was eager. "I have never heard that there is a law against black students."

"Don't make no trouble for yourself on our account, Ma'am. We can manage just fine. I can't believe we have such a fine place to live... .and all to ourselves too!"

"We will see about Eli, Esther. But, I agree that this is just right for you." Rose led them into the kitchen. It was spotless now. A small table stood in the middle of the floor, with three chairs pushed in around its edge. A kitchen range sat next to a tin sink, with a pump sitting next to it on a wooden counter.

"We have us two nice bedrooms too, and our own outhouse." Esther sounded pleased and proud of her new quarters.

Rose dropped the subject of school for Eli for now, but she resolved to pay a visit to the principal soon.

Dinner that night was a jolly affair. Rose and Michael insisted that Esther and Ben take their meals with them, and Eli and Joey were already friends.

Michael sat at the head of the table, and as they all joined hands for their blessing that they asked at each meal, he grinned. "It seems we are still working at fulfilling Uncle Andrew's wish for us to fill this house." He bowed his head. "We thank you, Lord for sending us this new family, and for all that you have bestowed upon us."

"Maybe you should remind him that all of our bedrooms are full now." Rose chuckled as she dipped up the first bowl of stew.

"Well, not really, Mama. We still have the loft." Andy grinned, and they all laughed.

1. The school on Liberty Street really did open in 1850, Rome's first public school to be financed by taxes.
2. Dominick Lynch did lay out a map of what he wanted his new investment to look like, and he did name some of the streets after himself and his family.
3. Mr. Rowley did take over publishing the paper in 1850 after working there since he was a boy.
4. There really was a fire in 1846 in Rome, resulting in the changes Andy told his family about.

Chapter FIVE

Eli Finds a Friend

"Isn't this a beautiful day!" Rose leaned over Susey's playpen to give her a cookie. She and Esther had just finished canning the last of the tomatoes picked from the big garden she and Michael and the children had planted after they arrived last June. Now it was the end of September, and most of the vegetables had been either canned, or put out in the root cellar for the long winter ahead. Michael and Ben were out picking apples from their orchard. Eli was picking up the apples that had fallen to the ground.

"It don't seem possible it will be cold before long – not when you look out at that sunshine." Esther agreed as she put clean dishes into a cupboard.

"I spoke to Mr. Thomas about the Board of Education Meeting they are holding tonight, and he promised they would vote on Eli going to school with the other children." Rose laughed. "He really did not know how to approach the issue. You and Ben and Eli are the only colored folk here in Rome, as far as he knows. No one has ever applied to go to school, at any rate."

Esther shook her head. "It seems too good to ever happen. Ben and me were lucky that our master was a good man. He taught both of us to read and write, and he let us get married when we grew up. Most owners

B. PETRIE
'03

34

back there where we came from make sure their slaves don't get any uppity notions like getting educated."

"Well, we will see how they vote. Eli has been learning Joey's lessons when they study after supper, so he should fit right in if they let him go."

"He has been going with Andy up to the newspaper office whenever I let him. Andy sure does like that Mr. Rowley, don't he?"

Rose nodded. After Esther and her family came to live with them Michael had agreed to let Andy work at the paper after school. Andy told them that Mr. Rowley was younger than him when he started working at the paper.

The paper was printed weekly but Andy ran errands for him almost every day and delivered papers to some of the customers who ordered them. Eli usually tagged after him when he could.

That afternoon Andy reported for work as soon as he changed out of his school clothes. Mr. Rowley watched him piling the folded papers into a bag.

"You have that right down to a system, young man. I think you have the makings of a good newsman." He smiled as he saw Andy's cheeks flush with pleasure at this compliment.

"I found out that if I separate the papers for customers west of the corner and deliver them first, I can come back and make a second load for the other direction, and do it quicker than I could if I try to drag all of them at once in a wagon." Andy slung the leather bag his father had helped him to make over his shoulder. "I will be back before long."

He looked around for Eli as he came out of the building. He had told Andy he would be around when he got his papers ready. He walked across the street to make his first delivery in Doctor Brown's Drug Store. The doctor was well known in Rome. Besides his medical practice he owned the store on the corner that was also the Post Office. Mail deliveries came every day now by train ever since those little stamps with the sticky glue had been issued in 1847.[1] Andy's heart always beat a little faster as he neared the store. Besides being one of the richest people in Rome, Doctor Brown was the father of the prettiest girl Andy had ever met. Sometimes she would be helping out in the store when he made his delivery. *She is here!* He could feel his cheeks redden as she turned from the counter, where she was filling a candy jar.

"Hello, Rachel." He cleared his throat, and silently cursed the way he blushed when he was embarrassed. Lately his voice cracked when he was nervous too. His father told him he was becoming a man, and men's voices changed as they got older. He wished it would hurry up and get finished changing.

"Hello, Andy." Rachel was blushing too, and that made him feel a little better. She was in Abby's grade, but she saw him in the hallway sometimes and she usually smiled at him shyly.

"I'm just delivering your paper." He took one out of his bag and put it on the counter.

"That little boy who lives at your house was in here a few minutes ago, looking for you. He said to tell you he was going down the block, but he would be seeing you while you are delivering your papers." She hesitated. "He is the only colored person I have ever talked to. He has a cute accent."

"His family came up from Virginia. I guess he has a southern accent. He is a good little kid. His mother and father work at our farm." Andy wished he could think of something else to say, but girls scared him, except for Abby and Kitty. "I guess I had better get along if I want to finish before supper."

She smiled. "I will probably see you in school tomorrow."

He was still feeling really good when he came to the end of the block and turned to go up Washington Street. There was an alley just before the Shamrock Bar, and as he started past it, he saw Eli leaning over a trash can. He stopped. "Eli?"

Eli looked up and motioned frantically for Andy to come into the alley. Andy approached him cautiously. Eli looked scared.

"What are you doing in this alley?" His eyes widened as he saw the crouched figure of a boy not much bigger than Eli. He was hunkered down between two cans filled with garbage. His face was a mass of bruises, and his shirt had been ripped almost off from his back. Blood was caked below his nose, and one eye was almost swollen shut. "What happened?"

"This here is Sam. His pa beat him up and he has taken off. The constable² is looking for him." Eli reached down to help the other boy up. "Tell Andy about it. He will help you.... You will, won't you?" His dark eyes were anxious.

"I don't know, Eli. Where is your mama"? He looked closely at the boy as he struggled to his feet. His clothes were filthy, and he smelled.

"I don't have no mama. There's just Pa and me.... and now he has gone too." Tears made streaks on his dirty face.

Andy didn't know what to do, so he did what came naturally to him. "Eli, take him down to the farm. Mama and Papa will know what we should do. At least they will help him clean up those bruises and give him something to eat."

"Yeah! Why didn't I think of that!" Eli nodded vigorously.

"Tell them that I will be home as soon as I finish delivering these papers." Andy watched Eli put his arm around the other boy, ignoring the way he smelled, and Sam went without protest.

Eli opened the door to the kitchen when he and Sam finally made it down the long dirt road, and the aroma of warm applesauce, simmering on the big black range, drifted out. He sighed in relief. *Mama and Miz Gleason will know what to do!*

"Eli! Who you got there?" His mother put down the stack of dishes she had been carrying to the table.

"This here is Sam Murphy, Ma. His pa hurt him and then he ran away. Andy said to bring him here."

Rose took one look at the boy's bruised face and ragged clothes, and her tender heart melted. "Eli, go and get Michael and your father. They will want to go to the police about this."

Sam stiffened at the mention of the police. "No! They will lock me up just like they do Pa!"

But Eli had already run out the door. When Michael and Ben came into the kitchen Rose was washing Sam's face with a warm cloth. She had set a pan of hot water, dipped from the range's warming reservoir, into the sink and she was carefully washing the blood and dirt away. She looked up at her husband with fire in her green eyes. "Did Eli tell you what happened to this boy?"

Michael tilted the boy's face gently to examine the damage. Now that the dirt was mostly gone, his blue eyes looked huge in his thin face. When he dropped his hand to his shoulder, the boy flinched away from him and Michael carefully turned him as he peeled the tattered shirt away.

"Oh! My God!" Rose covered her mouth with her hand, her eyes wide. Sam's thin back was criss-crossed with welts and dark bruises.

"Take care of him! I will be back." Michael's face was grim. His wife nodded. She knew he was going for the constable.

"Eli, you come with me and we will find him some clean clothes." Esther's voice was gentle. "Ben, bring the tub out so we can bathe him."

Rose turned to her wide-eyed children. "Supper may be a little late. Why don't you girls go in and light the lamps for me? Joey, you could go and help them."

When Michael came back with the constable, Eli and his mother had returned with clean pants and a soft shirt that hung on the boy's small frame. Rose had rubbed the raw sores with ointment and covered them with cloth. Now that he was clean, she saw that his hair was light brown and it waved all over his head. His lashes were long and curled around deep blue eyes. Except for his swollen eye and bruises, he was a truly beautiful child.

"Rose, this is Constable Stevens." Michael saw the little boy draw back behind his wife, his one good eye wide with fear. "There is nothing to be afraid of, son. The constable just wants to see that you are all right now."

The officer was a big Irishman, a father himself, and he looked at the bruises on Sam's face with a firm set to his mouth. "I arrested Rusty Murphy just last night. The only reason he is not in jail right now is that he told me there was no one to look after his son but him. Is that when he did this to you, lad?" He reached out to tilt Sam's chin so he could get a clearer look at him.

"He – he did some then. Are you going to take me to jail? I didn't do nothing. I was just in the alley looking for something to eat." Sam was trying hard not to cry again.

"No! You don't belong in jail." The big man shook his head sadly as he turned to Rose and Michael. "I will have to see if they have room for him at the county orphanage. Maybe I can take him home with me for the night."

"Wait a minute! Do you know what became of his father? Is he likely to come back for him?" Michael saw the scared look in the boy's eyes when his father was mentioned.

"Not likely. But I won't know where he is until I do some investigating."

Rose looked down at Sam's drawn face and fearful eyes. "He can stay here with us until everything is decided. Would you like that, Sam?" He nodded shyly.

"Would that be all right with you, Constable?" Michael saw the relief in the officer's face.

"That would give me a few days to find out just where we stand on this. He had been kneeling next to Sam, and he rose stiffly. "I will get back to you as soon as I can."

Rose stroked Sam's soft curly hair from his forehead. "No need to hurry. Sam will do just fine here with us."

*1. Stamps were issued in 1847 and Dr Brown did own a drugstore that served as a post office in 1850.
2. One constable was the only law enforcement officer in Rome in 1850, but more would be added shortly.*

Chapter SIX

And Now There Are Eight

The night that Sam came to them Michael and Ben brought one of the beds that were stored in the loft down to the room that Andy and Joey shared. By the time that he had been with them for two days there was a marked difference in him.

From the beginning he had no fear of Rose, but it took a day or two before he stopped flinching any time Michael got close. They decided not to send him to school until his bruises healed. He said that his father had never enrolled him in any school. He was eight-years-old, and he knew little about reading and writing, but it was amazing how he could add figures in his head. He sat with Eli and Joey when they did their lessons and if they made a mistake in adding or subtracting, he corrected them. When Rose asked him how he had learned so much about arithmetic, he said he knew how much it cost to eat in the places he went with his father, and he watched to see that they did not get cheated when his father was too drunk to know he was being charged too much.

Constable Stevens arrived the third day of Sam's stay, just after the other children had left for school. Rose had not heard from the Principal of the school, so Eli was home too. He and Sam were out in the stable when the constable came to the back door. One look at his face told Rose that his news was not good.

"Good Morning." She smiled at him. "Nothing can be as grim as your face would lead me to believe." She looked beyond him, and saw that Michael had seen him arrive. He was coming up the path behind him. Ben had the two boys with him, raking the area around the stable.

Michael shook hands as they all went inside. "Have we any coffee on the stove, Rose?" He turned to the officer. "Have a seat. It is always easier to talk sitting down with a cup of coffee in our hands. Don't you agree?"

The constable took the offered seat, but his face was still grim. "Nothing is going to make my news any easier. Sam's father got himself arrested in Utica the day he left here. He tried to hold up a store, and when the owner resisted, he beat him up. The man is in critical condition. It looks like he is going to be locked up for a long time – maybe for good if this man dies."

"Poor Sam! What now, Constable? What happens to the boy now?" Rose frowned as she poured their coffee.

"I can see if they have room for him over at the orphanage in Utica. His mother left about two years ago, according to Pat Sullivan, the bartender at the Shamrock. He let Sam and his father sleep in the back storage room of the bar because he felt sorry for the boy. Sam washes dishes out back and empties trash, things like that. When his father was sober, he did some cleaning too, but he has always been a mean son....excuse me!" His face was bright red when he realized he had almost cussed in front of Rose and Esther.

She chuckled. "I understand what you are telling us. There is no one in the village that Sam is related to that might take him in?"

"None that I can find. I guess the orphanage is our best bet, at least until his father gets out of jail."

"You would not permit that man to have Sam with him again! Would you?" Rose was indignant.

He looked uncomfortable. "It would probably be up to Judge Robinson."

Rose looked at her husband. He was turning his cup around and around. "How would it be if we just kept Sam here until you know how long his father will be gone?"

"That is probably going to be for a long time. If this man dies, Rusty, that's Sam's Pa, will be locked up for years before he could come back and claim the boy."

Rose had been standing behind them at the kitchen range, stirring a pot of chili sauce that she and Esther were going to can that day. "Sam can not go back with him! You saw his scars! She hesitated, looking at her husband first. "What if Michael and I ask to have custody of him, even if his father gets out of jail?"

"You would keep him permanently?" Stevens looked surprised. "You folks have a parcel of kids already!"

"There is always room for one more." Michael's voice was mild. "If you have no objection, we will keep him until such time as some member of his family makes a claim on him. In the meantime, we will register him in school."

The constable drained his cup. "That takes a load off from my shoulders. I hated the thought of trying to place that tike in the orphanage. They are overcrowded as it is." He rose, and looked over at the far end of the table where six loaves of bread were cooling on a rack. He grinned. "I told my Mary how good your kitchen smelled when I was here before. Darned it don't smell even better today, with that chili sauce cooking and the bread adding to it."

"Let me give you a loaf to take home." Rose spoke impulsively. "Esther, can you find me some wrapping in the pantry?"

"It looks like we have added another member to our family." Michael watched the constable walk up the drive, his loaf of bread carefully tucked under one arm. "You know, Ben and I have been talking. We have been up and down those loft steps so often these past months, it might be a good idea to make a change upstairs. We could make a stairway, and add another story to the house. It would be a simple matter to finish the loft."

Rose laughed. "You are not thinking we might enlarge the family any more, are you?"

He grinned. "We agreed that whatever the good Lord sees fit to give us, we will accept." His face sobered. "Actually, our rooms upstairs are full. What if some of the family wants to visit? It would be nice to have the extra space. Our work outside should be slowing down now and we could take the time to do the work."

When he had left them to go outside, Esther smiled at Rose. A few months ago she would not have offered an opinion, but now they were friends. "You got no problem with having all these children? I never see you sit down."

"No. I love them. The only thing that worries me is making ends meet. With the taxes we pay to keep the children in school, and the cost of clothing them, we could use some extra income." She looked thoughtful. "You know, Esther, I have baked cakes and pies for neighbors. What would you think of selling them at a store?"

"All the time?" Esther looked surprised.

"Yes." Rose laughed. "While Ben and Michael are redoing our upstairs, we could go into business here in my kitchen. We could be partners. What do you think?"

"My Lord! Let's do it!" Esther was a good head taller than Rose, and much bigger. She grabbed her around the waist and danced her around the table. "Shall we tell Ben and Michael?" "Yes!" They each grabbed a shawl, and ran out to join their husbands.

Chapter SEVEN

Settling In

"Something smells good." Michael sniffed as he opened the door to the back stairway. "When you get time to stop a minute, Rose would you and Esther like to come up and see what Ben and I have been up to?"

Rose was just taking two pies from the beehive oven, and she carried them to the racks spread out on the long kitchen table. A row of freshly baked bread cooled on two of the racks, and Esther was loading the floor of the oven with hot coals from the fireplace pit to preheat it for the tray of cookies she and Rose had just finished dropping by spoonfuls onto a tin. A row of pheasants were slowly turning on the spit over the fireplace pit, and an iron kettle full of chili that was nestled in the coals below it was sending its fragrance into the air.

"Now would be a good time, while the oven re-heats." Rose looked at Esther. "Don't you agree"

"I do." Esther brushed her hands together to free them of the flour she had dusted on them when she flattened the cookies. They followed Michael up the stairs to the upper hall. Rose had been surprised how well the new stairway fit into the back area of the hall. Three wide stairs led to a landing at the left wall, and turned right to reach another landing ten steps up.

There it opened onto the newly finished third floor.

"We decided to make two rooms up here, with built-in cupboards and bunk beds. How do you like this first one?" Michael stood back, his hands on his hips, as he watched Rose's reaction to this addition to their house.

She clasped her hands. "Oh, I love it! Don't you, Esther?" Rose surveyed the big, pine-paneled room. The floor was made of wide planks, joined by wooden dowels, and along the far side wall three beds had been built at even intervals. Between each of them was a wardrobe for clothes. At the end of each bed a flat-topped desk was pushed against the foot-board, and a stool that fit snugly underneath it stood ready for use. A big double window at one end looked out on the fields in back of the house.

"This is wonderful!" Esther clapped her hands together. "Looks like we had better get those feather ticks finished right quick! What do you want to bet that Andy, Joey and Sam won't want to move right in here?"

Michael laughed. "My thoughts exactly! And I think it is a good idea. If we have company, they would probably be more comfortable on the second floor."

"While we were doing this room, Michael said we might as well finish up another room at the front here." Ben pointed at the doorway that had been cut into the wall, and they walked across to look into another room that had just as much space as the one they were in.

Rose laughed. "You are not thinking our family could grow again, are you?"

"Land sakes! Seven youngsters ought to be enough for anyone!" Esther chuckled.

"You might as well say eight young 'uns....Eli is

over here with them most of the time." Ben added.

"He still finds it hard to believe he is going to school. It was mighty nice of Mr. Thomas to make the school board see that he was taken in." Esther wiped her eyes with a corner of her long apron as a tear trickled down her cheek.

"He is such a smart little boy. He is helping Sam to catch up with the rest of them. Sam hates being in with the twins, but it will not be long before he will move up a grade." Rose sniffed. "I smell something! It must be those cakes I have in the oven." She turned to start down the steps. "Why don't you two men come down and have a sandwich?"

She took the three cake layers out of the oven while Esther made room for the four of them to sit at the other end of the long table.

"Have you a sale for all of this?" Michael looked at the baked goods spread out across from him.

"Yes. Mr. Wilson says he will take this same order every week day. He says people are waiting for them every afternoon."

"Joey, Eli and Sam are busy after school with your new brood of chickens and Chocolate." Michael grinned. "Where did they ever come up with that name for a cow, I wonder?"

"That is easy....Eli said she is the same color as the chocolate cakes we make." Esther smiled as she started to spread frosting on one of the cake layers. "All the boys agreed it was a good name."

The back door opened, letting in a blast of cold air as the children all came in from school. Rose had a kiss for each of them, and Esther handed them one of the cookies she had just taken from the oven.

"I have to hurry! Mr. Rowley has some special

deliveries he wants me to make." Andy grabbed a handful of cookies on his way up the stairs.

"Sarah said her father will be home this weekend. November this year is really cold. The canal is freezing over in some places." Abby drank the last of her milk. "Are we really going to have Minnie, Maude and Molly boarding with us this winter, Papa?"

"It looks that way. If Sarah really thinks they will be coming in that soon, you boys had better plan on helping us prepare their stalls. Doctor Anderson has already spoken for the other spare stall we have out there. With our own two mares, the barn will be full."

"Might be you will want to add on next spring." Ben chewed thoughtfully on a moist cookie.

"Hey! Pa, this is great!" Andy came bounding down the stairs. "I just went up to see the loft. Can Joey and Sam and I sleep up there?"

His father laughed. "We are considering that. Why don't you boys go up and see what you think of the idea?" He rose and stretched. "Come on, Ben, let's put the finishing touches on, shall we?"

Joey grabbed his hand as they started up the stairs, his short legs pumping to keep up with him. Rose watched them with a catch in her throat. Joey's love for Michael always made her realize how lucky they were to have him. He had never really known his own father. She absently smoothed Sam's brown waves off his forehead, marveling again at how beautiful his blue eyes were. While Joey clung to Michael, this little one turned to her, and she felt her heart warm with an answering love.

Esther, standing at the fireplace, checking the roasting fowl, silently thanked the Lord for bringing her family to this farm.

Chapter EIGHT

And Two Makes Ten

"Papa! Here they come!" Abby came running down the back stairs. "Sarah is with them, and her mother too."

Michael rose from the table where he had been having a mid-morning cup of coffee. It was Saturday, and he was glad that the stalls for Fairweather's mules were ready.

"Is that Jack with them?" Kitty asked excitedly, hoping no one noticed she was blushing. She felt her heart beat a little faster lately whenever she saw him. "No, he looks too thin. And he doesn't have Jack's dark hair." She pushed her own hair back nervously.

Abby laughed. She'd guessed that Kitty had a crush on Jack. "Maybe Jack found something better to do at home this morning," she teased. "Oh no, there he is! Just behind that first boy, and there is another smaller one…. But of course he isn't as handsome as Jack either, is he, Kitty?"

Kitty ignored her as she ran to the front door and squinted, trying to see more clearly as they approached.

"Yes! It is Jack! He is leading Minnie, I think, and you are right, there is another boy with him." Kitty giggled as they both hurried out to the porch.

Rose brought their jackets out with her, and wrapped her own shawl around her shoulders as she waved to

Abigail. "Come in! It is freezing out here!"

Abigail and Sarah ran the last few steps and came into the wide hall as Rose stepped back inside. "It is cold! I think we are going to have an early winter."

"Who are those boys with Jack?" Abby was sure she had never seen them in school.

"Um….just two boys Papa brought home with him. They are helping with the mules until they get settled into their stalls." Sarah looked at her mother, and Abigail shook her head slightly.

"Your father will be in shortly. He will introduce Jess and Jamie to everyone then."

Something about the way she hesitated made Kitty and Abby look at each other. *She has a secret. Something is going on!*

Rose led them out to the warm kitchen. Now that cold weather had arrived, the front rooms were kept closed unless they had company. When that happened, the big fireplaces in each room were lit. Upstairs, each bedroom had a small pot-bellied wood stove to take the chill away, but the warm kitchen had become the place where they gathered.

"Sit down and have a hot cup of coffee to warm you. Abby, Kitty, why don't you girls bring out a plate of cookies."

"No baking today, Rose?" Abigail had become accustomed to seeing the table full of pies and bread when she visited.

"Not on Saturday. This is our family day. We bake enough on Friday to carry us through the weekend." Rose laughed. "It is the only day that Esther has to clean her own place."

The girls set plates of cookies on the table and took cups from the cupboards.

"I imagine you are happy to have John home. Has the canal closed for the winter?"

"Pretty much, although there are still a few barges who try to get in an extra trip or two." Abigail took a sip of hot coffee. "I wish John could stay home all winter. He is going to rest until Thanksgiving, but then he and Dan will have to get ready to leave right after Christmas. They signed a contract to cut lumber up north somewhere near Boonville and Woodgate to haul next spring."

The back door opened and Michael came in first, holding it open for John and his brother, Dan. As they entered, he beckoned to the two boys that Kitty and Abby had spied earlier. "This is Jess and his brother, Jamie. Come in where it is warm boys."

A thin boy, with shaggy blond hair, edged his way into the room, and his dirty hands twisted a cap as he looked down at his feet. He was dressed in a pair of overalls that were too big for him, and his jacket was threadbare. The other boy, who was much smaller, was dressed like him, and he kept trying to get behind his bigger brother.

They look scared to death! Rose smiled at them as she came over and kissed John and his brother on their bearded cheeks before she turned to the boys. "Are you boys hungry? We are just having cookies and milk." She pointed to the table where the girls had placed a pitcher of foaming milk that she had skimmed only an hour before.

Neither boy answered, only shaking their heads. Neither of them looked up to meet her eyes.

"I brought the boys with me from Albany. I just told Michael that I found them stowed away in the bow-stable after we were well underway," John explained. "They

53

told me that they ran away from the orphanage there. They lost their father two years ago and their mother died this summer. The authorities put them into the orphanage because there was no family to take them."

"How awful!" Rose went over to the boys and lifted Jamie's chin with her finger. His brother was tall, and his solemn, dark eyes reminded her of a wounded deer. Jamie and he had a strong family resemblance. Her voice was gentle. "You didn't like it at the orphanage?"

Jamie shook his head. "No! That Mrs. O'Brien was mean! She shut me in a closet because I missed my Ma, and I was crying. She said she didn't like crybabies." He swiped at his eyes with a dirty hand. "She took a belt to Jess when he tried to let me out."

Jess looked defiant. "All Jamie and me has got is each other, and no one is going to be mean to him or separate us! That old witch said she was going to put him up for adoption, and she said I was too old, so I could stay and work for her until I was full grown."

"How old are you, Jess?" Michael placed a hand on his shoulder, and he jerked away.

"I am fifteen. Jamie is ten." He looked scared. "You are not going to send us back, are you? Are you going to turn us over to the cops?"

"I told the boys that you sometimes take children in, but I can see that you may not have room for them. I would take them myself, but our house has only two small bedrooms, and I have to be gone for most of the winter." Captain John shook his head. "I don't know where else to turn."

"We could sleep in the barn, and we don't eat much. We could help out around here. This is a big place. You must have lots of work." Jamie's dark eyes were full of tears.

Rose looked at Michael, and he grinned, knowing what she was thinking. He raised his eyebrows. "The loft?"

She smiled. "Uncle Andrew would never believe this!"

Chapter NINE

Company Coming

Susey banged on the tray of her highchair. "Cookie, Mama!"

Rose laughed. "No cookies this early in the day, little one. How about a nice piece of bread and butter?"

Esther chuckled as she watched Rose cut the bread and put it on Susey's tray. "She sure does talk plain for a baby." She placed a bowl of freshly churned butter on the table and took the empty one from Rose. "With all of these young 'uns to feed, it is a good thing your Michael got you that cow and all of them chickens."

Rose nodded. "It is. And that big turkey he brought home from Mr. Williams farm, when he took Jess over to talk about working there, will do just fine for Thanksgiving. With one of the hams we just put out in the smokehouse, and the cheese round that Jess brought home, we should have a wonderful holiday meal."

"It makes it nice that Mr. Williams hired our Jess to help him make cheese after school.[1] He has some sons of his own helping out, don't he?" Esther asked.

"Yes, but he says he can use the extra help. He told Michael that his cheese business has really grown since he started it. They are enlarging the building where they process the cheese, and he plans to start buying milk from all of the surrounding farmers so they can ship their cheese." Rose laughed. "He plans to take his sons into the business now that they are expanding. His wife said she was glad to have Jess there to help too, and Jess says he is going to take his brother with him sometimes when they are extra busy."

"It don't seem possible that it is time for Thanksgiving already! It seems like only yesterday that we got here." Esther shook her head in wonder as she briskly kneaded the dough on the floured surface of the table where she was working.

Rose chuckled. " I don't know what my brother is going to think when he sees how big my family has grown since I last saw him. He and Jane have two servants in their New York City apartment." Her face sobered. "He is all the family I have, you know. My father and mother have been gone for over ten years now, and Steve took over Papa's business. He still buys most of the wool for his factory from Scotland, like Papa did. I was surprised that he and Jane decided to make the trip just now."

"You and Michael have made this farm into a real home for all of us. It looks mighty fine, and you are as ready as you can be for the winter ahead of us, and for your company." Esther looked around the big kitchen approvingly. "Your brother and his family will have to think you have done right well for yourself."

Rose sighed. "I hope that you are right. Jane and I never had much in common. She grew up in England, and her folks had a lot of money. She and my brother met when he was on a buying trip with my father in England. She is accustomed to much grander things. She did not think much of the little place Michael and I had in Amsterdam."

"You have done a fine job of finishing this place.

The company parlor and the library and dining room, and that little office you made for Michael, look grand. And your bedrooms are real nice. Don't you worry. Your family will like all of it." Esther's voice was firm.

Rose laughed. "I hope they like children! I have not told them about our new family. I just didn't know how to explain the way the children came to us. Michael and I decided to wait and let them meet when they get here. Their two daughters are thirteen and fourteen, and little Steve is about Jamie's age."

"Don't you worry your pretty head. Everything will be just fine." Esther gave the mound of bread dough a final pat. "When they get here Saturday we will be ready for them."

Rose chuckled. "But the real question is, will they be ready for us? When the children are all in school like they are today, it does not seem possible that so much has changed since we arrived last June."

"It is a good thing Michael and Ben finished that loft when they did. With your brother and his family coming for the holiday, you would not have had room for them otherwise."

"Yes. Steve and Jane can use the spare room, and his two girls can sleep in with Abby. Steven can bunk in with Jess and Jamie in the loft." She looked around her kitchen with pride, as she added, "You are right, Esther, they will love this place just as much as we do." She laughed and crossed her fingers…."I hope!"

1. *It is true that Jesse Williams and his wife, Amanda had a cheese business in Rome during this time.*

Chapter TEN

Trouble in the Air?

Michael straightened up and stretched as he watched Eli, Joey and Sam come running out to the barn. They had just come home from school and changed their clothes, and they were eating a thick slice of fresh bread spread with strawberry jam as they ran across the frosty lawn and drive. Sam was cramming the last bite in his mouth as they arrived at the barn, and Michael was struck again by the boy's insecurity.

He eats every meal as though he is not sure there will be another one coming his way. He stooped to give him a hug. Joey, jealous of anyone who took Michael's attention away from him, waited his turn eagerly. Ben swung Eli up in the air before setting him back on his feet.

"You boys ready to exercise the mules?"

Inside the barn, Minnie twitched her long ears as she watched. *It is about time! I get tired of standing inside this stable all day! I hate to admit it, but I miss my walk along the canal.* She snorted and pawed the straw beneath her feet.

The two men came into the barn with the boys and showed them how to adjust the halters on the three mules so they could fasten the reins that would be used to lead them.

B. PETRIE
'08

"Take them out into the south pasture and give them a good walk. We may not be able to do that all winter if we get too much snow, but for now it is good for them."

You are right! This fresh air makes me want to kick up my heels! Minnie kicked her hind feet and neighed.

Joey jumped back, but then he laughed as Minnie lowered her head and butted him gently.

Molly followed Sam as he set out at a brisk jog, and Maude snorted when Eli pulled on her lead so that they could keep up with the others.

Michael laughed as he and Ben watched them make the first circuit of the fenced pasture. "That will keep them busy while we clean the stalls. The exercise is good for all of them. The boys have been cooped up in school all day, and the mules have been closed up in the stable."

He and Ben made quick work of cleaning the stalls, and as they swept the aisle clean, he looked over at the two mares in the last three stalls. "I am glad we finished the corral last week. The horses are a handful. I wonder whether the boys could control them. When the weather turns we will probably turn the mules into the corral too. Doctor Andrews likes this arrangement. He should be bringing his old Betsy in after he finishes his rounds to visit his patients."

"Esther says your brother-in-law and his family will be coming in on the train Saturday." Ben chuckled. "We're sure going to have a house-full for over Thanksgiving, ain't we?"

Michael nodded. "Yes, we are! I hope they will adapt." He shook his head. "They are accustomed to city living, and their children are pretty much taken care of by a Nanny that has been with them since they were born."

The two men turned as they heard the boys bringing the mules back into the stable. Each boy filled the manger for one of the mules before they left to go in and wash up for supper.

Now that was a nice change! I am glad the Captain is leaving us here for the winter. Molly snorted as she looked over at her sisters.

Did you girls hear someone in the barn late last night? I am sure there was someone creeping around back by the doors. It was so dark that I couldn't make anything out, but I know I heard the back door creaking. Minnie shook her head nervously.

I sleep so sound since we are off the canal. You probably just heard mice in the oat bin. Molly neighed.

Maybe, but I think I will keep one eye open for as long as I can tonight. I keep thinking of that mean Mike when we were on the canal. Minnie chewed her oats thoughtfully.

Rose looked around the circle of rosy faces as all of the children gathered around the table a little later. "When I sent you out this morning to bring in the milk for breakfast, did you see the bowl of stew that was left yesterday, Andy?"

He shook his head. "No. Where did you put it out there?"

"It was on the shelf your Papa made for me, just inside the door to the ice house." She frowned. "I went looking for it to add to our meal tonight, and I couldn't find it."

"Maybe it got spilled and the dish rolled under the shelf," Michael suggested.

"Of course, that is probably what happened." She shrugged lightly. "I will look tomorrow and clean up the mess." They all clasped hands, and she looked at

Joey. "Is it your turn tonight to say the blessing?"

"Yes..." He thought for a minute. "Thank you God for these new benches Uncle Michael and Ben made. I haven't found a splinter in my back side yet!"

Michael chuckled, and then tried to look serious as Rose shook her head at the little boy. "Not too good, young man. Just for that it will be your turn again tomorrow."

Chapter ELEVEN

Mysterious Happenings

Rose looked up from stirring the kettle in front of her as Jess and Jamie came into the kitchen. "Good morning! Jess, would you go out to the ice house and bring me in a pitcher of milk, and a bowl of eggs? I want to get breakfast out of the way as soon as we can. The train will be coming in early this afternoon, and I want to have everything ready for our company."

Jess took his jacket, a warm fleece lined one that had replaced his shabby old coat, and shrugged into it, loving its warm feel. "Come on, Jamie, you can help. We need to eat so we can get over to Mr. Williams. He has a big shipment of cheese going out today."

Jamie silently followed his brother out the door as he threw his own new coat around his shoulders.

Esther shook her head. "That boy is still mighty troubled. It ain't natural for him to stick so close to his brother all the time."

Rose sighed. "You are right. It takes some children longer than others to get over the death of someone they loved. I am glad that Amanda Williams spoke to her husband after she and I talked about how Jamie withdraws from everyone when his brother is not with him. He is going to let Jamie work with Jess over there until he feels more secure here." She chuckled.

"He and Amanda have such big hearts they always find room for children, just like we do. Amanda says the boys are a big help to them."

"They do a right good business making cheese, don't they?" Esther laughed. "About as good as we do with our baked goods."

Rose nodded. "Yes. They plan to expand next year so that they can ship to a bigger market. We are in a wonderful spot, being so close to the canal and to the Mohawk River.... and the railroad line." She looked up as the two boys came in the back door.

"There were only a few eggs in the bowl. You must have used them all when you baked yesterday." Jess set the big pottery bowl on the table.

Rose frowned. "I was sure there were at least two dozen eggs in that bowl."

"Well, they are not out there now. Are they, Jamie?" Jess turned to his brother.

"No. Jess and I both looked." Jamie went to the sink and pumped a basin full of water to wash in.

As they moved to sit at the table, the other children drifted down to the kitchen too.

Rose and Esther dipped bowls of warm porridge and added a platter of warm biscuits.

"I guess we will have to do without bacon and eggs this morning." Rose kept her tone light, but she was worried. In the past week she had found food missing from the outbuildings almost every day. *I wonder if one of the children is not getting enough to eat and feels he has to steal food?* She looked around the table. Susey was in her highchair where Kitty had placed her. Her big blue eyes shone with happiness as she bit into a warm biscuit.

They all look happy.... Except maybe Jamie. But there

is no reason for him to take food. There is always plenty here in the kitchen.

The back door opened and Michael and Ben came in, bringing a gust of cold air with them. Michael grinned as he looked around the table, listening to their chatter as they all planned what they were going to do that day. "No eggs and bacon this morning?" He looked over at his wife as he raised his eyebrows. "Are we saving it for our company?"

She laughed. "No. It seems I miscounted when I finished baking yesterday. I thought I had almost a bowl full of eggs, but the boys only found a few this morning."

Eli had come in with his father. "I put almost a full bowl of eggs on the shelves when we collected them after school. Did you and Ma use them last night?"

Rose frowned. "No. I guess I will have to take a closer look out there after breakfast."

"Did you find that bowl of stew you missed?" Michael finished his bowl of cereal. *I wonder if we have someone breaking into our supplies. With the canal closing there are a lot of men out of work for the winter. I will have to talk to Ben and see if we can come up with some way to be certain we lock our out-buildings every night.*

"I went out to look, but I never found it." Rose shook her head, warning him not to frighten the children.

"We all forget things sometimes." Michael looked around the table at the rosy cheeks of the children. "Our company will be arriving before long. Has everyone done their chores? All the bedrooms ready for out guests to see them?" He laughed. "We want to impress them, you know. None of them have ever been here before."

There was a chorus of assurances that everything was just waiting for the arrival of Andy and Abby's cousins and their parents.

The train would arrive at the depot at one o'clock that afternoon, and long before that the house was ready for them. Rose and Michael had decided to meet the train alone. Her family would meet the children when they arrived at the farm.

She could feel the butterflies in her stomach as she watched the big engine approach. She had not seen her brother, Steven or his wife for well over a year.

Chapter TWELVE

City Cousins

Steve was the first one off the train, and he turned to help his wife down from the high step. Her blonde hair was swept back in the latest style, and her blue velvet traveling costume matched the color of her eyes. Steven turned to help his daughters, and they stepped down as daintily as their mother had. Behind them, Stevie grinned at his aunt and uncle, and jumped the last step to the ground.

Rose hurried forward to be hugged with enthusiasm by her tall brother, and turned to kiss Jane's cheek as Michael shook hands with his brother-in-law. Their oldest daughter, Katy, was dark like her father and little brother, but Amy, a year younger than Katy, was a small replica of her mother.

Katy rushed forward to hug her aunt, and Stevie hurled himself into Michael's arms, but Amy walked sedately forward to kiss Rose coolly on the cheek, just as her mother had done.

"I cannot wait to get to your estate and wash the grime of this awful railroad off!" Jane brushed at her full skirts.

"Actually, the train service has improved a lot this past year." Michael grinned. "And *farm* is more the word you are looking for, Jane. Estate does not describe our holdings." He leaned down to peck his sister-in-law's cheek. He always thanked his lucky stars that Rose was Jane's complete opposite.

"This is really quite....*rural!*" Amy looked with disdain at the wide dirt road where their carriage waited.

"Oh, Rome has really grown lately. We are still a village, but there is serious talk of someday merging with the Town of Rome so we can become a city." Michael was watching their luggage being unloaded on the platform. *Three trunks and two cases? I wonder how long they plan to stay?*

Ben drove up in the flatbed wagon as they talked. He and Michael had decided they would need it for the luggage.

"You have a slave?" Jane's face registered her surprise. "I didn't think they were common up here in the North."

"Ben is my hired hand. He is a free man." Michael's voice was firm. "I don't know what I would do without him. He and his wife, Esther, and their little boy have been with us almost from the time we arrived."

"Esther and I run the house and Michael and Ben run the barns." Rose laughed. "And we all manage the children."

"How nice." Jane stood stiffly as she watched Ben's lanky form approach.

"Looks like we have a real load, Ben." Michael greeted him with a grin and a wink. "If you want to bring the wagon closer, I will give you a hand." He walked over to the pile of luggage as Ben moved the wagon into the parking area.

"How long these folks plan to be here?" Ben scratched his head and whispered as he grinned at Michael. "Look like they might be moving in?"

70

"Just over Thanksgiving, I believe." Michael tried not to laugh as he leaned to help Ben lift the first trunk. He lowered his voice. "I like Steven, but I can take Jane only in small doses."

It took only a few minutes to drive the short distance from the railroad to the wide dirt road leading to the farm.

"Oh, this is really quite a spread!" Steven smiled at his sister as they drove down the wide drive to the house. Now that the maple trees were bare, the full impact of the big farmhouse was before them. The grounds had been groomed this past summer and fall, and the outbuildings had been freshly painted. Looking south, their orchards spread beyond the big corral where Doctor Anderson's horse and the three mules were spending the sunny afternoon.

"This is really quite nice." Jane smiled as she took her husband's hand while she dismounted from the carriage.

Katy and Amy climbed down next, and Rose could not help smiling as she saw Amy wrinkle her nose as a breeze brought the earthy odor of the stables and animals to them. *I am afraid Amy is not going to be thrilled during her stay.*

"Come in. The girls have prepared a snack for you, and I am sure you will want to freshen up. There is warm water in the basins in your rooms, and clean towels." Rose and Michael went with them to the front door while Ben took the wagon and carriage out to the barns.

There was a fragrant wood smell in the wide hall as they entered. Fires burned in every room on either side of the entryway, and competed with the smell of furniture polish on the gleaming wide stair rails of the front stairway, seldom used by the family. Rose looked with satisfaction into the rooms she had so lovingly redecorated since their arrival.

"We laid out a lunch in the kitchen. It is the warmest room in the house during the winter." She could feel her relatives eyes taking in the rooms that they passed.

"Say, this is nice!" Her brother stood with his hands on his hips, looking at the big kitchen. The trestle table that was long enough to comfortably seat their large family shone from frequent polishing and scrubbing. The long deacon benches that Michael and Ben had replaced their chairs with, gleamed too, and the black range had been polished to a high luster. Michael had applied coat after coat of varnish to the kitchen's wide oak planked floor, making it easier for Rose to keep it clean, and a small rag rug stood before the big fireplace. The aroma of fresh bread and apple pie filled the air, and the table had been laid with Rose's best china. Esther looked up with a wide smile as she put the last touches to the table.

"This is Esther, my good friend, and my right hand! Esther, this is my brother and his wife, Jane, that I told you about." She turned to the others, "And this is Katy, Amy and Stevie."

"I am pleased to meet you! Rose has been working for a week to get this place ready for you."

"We had lunch before we went to fetch you, so as soon as you meet the family, we will let you sit down and eat. I know you must be famished." Rose's voice was calm, but she could feel the knot in her stomach tighten. After seeing her sophisticated family again she was almost afraid for them to meet the children.

"I cannot wait to see Andy and Abby again!" Katy was excited.

"They are eager to see you too." Michael went to the back stairway and opened the door. "Company is here! Everyone downstairs!" He stepped back as he heard the thunder of approaching feet.

Andy was first, followed closely by Joey, Sam and Eli. Just behind them, came Abby, with Meggie holding her hand. Kitty followed close on her heels, carrying Susey. They had all changed into school clothes in honor of their company, and Rose felt a catch in her throat as she looked with pride at their shining faces.

Katy was the first to react. She rushed forward to hug her cousin Andy, and then Abby. "I was afraid this was going to be a dull visit here in the country, but it looks like we are having a party."

Andy grinned. "No party. Just family. Let me introduce you!" He went down the line, naming each one, and ending with Susey.

"Mama!" Susey reached out to Rose, and she laughed as she took her into her arms.

"Andy is right. As you can see, our family has grown!"

"These are all your children? Where did you get them?" Her brother looked bewildered, but he smiled uncertainly.

"It is a long story, but yes, these are all our children, and there are two more who will be home later this afternoon."

She glanced at Jane, who stood stiffly next to her husband, and Amy moved to stand next to her. Neither of them had said a word. Stevie was gazing in amazement at the group before him, and his eyes came to rest on Eli. "He is colored! You have a colored boy?" His question was innocent, and it was one that Eli had become accustomed to hearing. He answered for himself.

"My name is Eli. This is my mama, and my pa is out putting the animals in the stable, but I belong here too. Don't I, Aunt Rose?" He turned with complete confidence to her.

"You are a very important member of our family." She ruffled his dark curls before turning back to her brother and his family. "How our family got so big is a story for tonight, but right now let us take you up to your rooms so you can freshen up. The boys will bring your luggage in."

Chapter THIRTEEN

The Plot Thickens!

When Michael took Steve out to the barns to show him around, Jane said she needed a nap after her long journey. Rose breathed a sigh of relief as she watched her leave the kitchen to take the front stairs to the second floor. Abby and Kitty took Meggie with them when they went to settle Susey for a nap, and invited Amy and Katy to join them in Abby's room where they would be sleeping during their visit. Jess and Jamie had come in from work, and were up in the loft changing their clothes when the other boys took Steven with them to show him where he would be sleeping.

Esther briskly stacked dishes in the wooden dry-sink. "We got ourselves quite a house-full! It is a good thing the young'uns got this next week off from school because of the holiday."

"Yes. That will help." Rose smiled ruefully. "Jane and I do not have a lot in common, I'm afraid. I hope we can entertain them while they are here."

"How long do you suppose they plan to stay? By the looks of the trunks Ben and Michael just took upstairs, it looks like a long visit." Esther watched Rose wipe the dishes and place them on the table, ready for the next meal. A pot-roast was already simmering on the black range. Everything had been prepared ahead for today's meals and tomorrow's. Sunday was always a relaxed day at the farm. After church a hearty lunch was served, and the leftovers usually made a cold supper.

"They told us they were coming for Thanksgiving, so they will be here for a least all of this next week. Jane always carries a lot of luggage when she travels." She hesitated. "I was surprised that they made the long trip from New York City just now because usually Steve goes to Scotland to order new fabrics at this time of year, and Jane always goes with him. They leave the children with their Nanny." She laughed. "I am sure the children will enjoy themselves though this week. Did you notice that Jamie and Steven seemed to like each other? Maybe Jamie is finally feeling more at home."

Jess watched his brother showing Steven his desk where he did his homework. Their front room was just like the one that the other three boys shared. Jess still had a hard time believing that Rose and Michael seemed to really want them, but he had to admit they really seemed to like kids, and he loved being part of their family. He looked over at his brother and Steven. *Maybe Jamie is feeling good about being here too.*

Abby sat on the edge of the single bed that had been moved into her room and she watched her cousins unpack some of their things. "Mama thought maybe you girls would like to sleep together. If you do, you can have my bed and I will sleep on this one."

"I could not possibly sleep with anyone! I have to have my own bed!" Amy looked horrified at the notion of sleeping with her sister.

"You can have this bed, and I'll sleep with Katy." Abby giggled. "Is that okay with you, Katy?"

Katy laughed. "I wouldn't want to give Amy any of

my germs. As long as you don't take all the covers, we should have no problem."

"Let's go and get Kitty and Meggie. Susey will sleep for a least an hour, and we can go out to the stables and visit with Minnie, Molly and Maude." Abby jumped up, and Katy clapped her hands.

"That sounds like fun. Come on, Amy."

"You want to go out to that smelly barn? Not me! I'll just lie down and rest for a while like Mother is doing." Amy sat on the side of the single bed, then laid back on the new pillows. "This is not very comfortable, but I guess it will do."

Out in the blacksmith's orderly shop, Steve admired the rows of equipment, and the furnace that Michael used to temper his iron. "You have quite a setup here!" He sank down onto a wooden stool as Michael moved around, putting tools away until Monday. He hesitated. "I must admit it was quite a shock to see all of the children you and Rose have taken in. Jane and I made this trip to see how you were doing. We wanted to make you a proposition." He laughed, a little nervously.

"A proposition?" Michael raised an eyebrow.

"Yes. We are planning to take an extended trip to Europe. We want to expand our business, and it means that we will have to be away for several months." He cleared his throat. "I know it is a lot to ask, now that you have all of these other children, but we hoped you would let the girls and Stevie stay here with you while we are gone." He saw the stunned look on Michael's face, and added hastily, "Of course we would plan to pay you for the extra expenses you will have. I just do not feel comfortable leaving them alone with the servants for that length of time….and Jane insists on going with me."

That is what all of the luggage is for! Michael did not know how to react. He loved his nieces and nephew, even Amy, in spite of the fact that she had most of Jane's less than endearing traits. But three more children? He raised his eyes to the heavens. *I will bet you are up there laughing, Uncle Andrew!* He chuckled. "Well, this ought to make for some good conversation tonight. Do your children realize what you plan? And, of course Rose has to agree, you know."

Rose calmly accepted her brother's request, and like Michael, she laughed as she told Steve about Uncle Andrew's wish that they fill the house with children. "I just hope that he realizes that there is no more room if we do this! She looked at her brother a bit doubtfully as they sat at the kitchen table drinking coffee while the rest of the family was still outside or upstairs. "How do the girls and Stevie feel about staying with us for a long period of time?"

Her brother looked uncomfortable. "We haven't told them. You know how Jane is. She feels that children need to accept their parents' wishes, and she didn't want to deal with any problem they might have with the arrangement – particularly with Amy."

"I see." Rose looked at Michael. "Well, this calls for a family conference tonight. Everyone has to agree or this will not work. You both see that?"

Chapter FOURTEEN

Trouble at the Farm

Minnie pawed the straw beneath her feet. She was restless. Every night she was awakened by unusual noises at the back of the stable, and tonight, since the weather had turned very cold and noises sounded louder, she could hear stealthy footsteps near her. The door creaked, and stealthy sounds over her head in the barn's loft made her wake her sisters tonight. They were impatient with her when she disturbed their sleep.

I am sure someone is sneaking around in here and I don't like it! She shook her head and her ears twitched. *There! I hear someone at the back door!* Footsteps creeping closer scared her and she neighed loudly.

"Shut up!" A voice snarled just behind her, and a hand reached to snatch her blanket from her back.

You give that back! I need it to keep me warm! Minnie snorted and reared up.

Inside the little house just behind the stable, Eli shook his father's shoulder. "Pa, I hear noises out in the stable again!"

This was not the first time he had done this in the past two weeks, and Ben was impatient.

"I told you before, Eli, I went out and looked when you heard noises, and no one is out there. You just hear

the animals moving around. Now, go back to sleep!"

"No, Pa! This is different! I heard one of the mules real loud."

"Okay! Just this once more I am going to go and look, but I have to tell you, this is the last time." Ben got out of bed and groggily pulled his pants on, sliding his suspenders over his undershirt.

"Listen, Pa!" Eli tugged on his father's arm and his brown eyes were wide.

"He is right! I hear them too." Esther, wakened by their voices, sat up and reached for her robe. By this time the other animals had joined Minnie pawing and snorting.

The three of them shivered in the cold night air as they went to the back door of the stable and Ben held his big lantern high so he could see. "What is this?" He saw Minnie crowding a big man against the wall of her stall. Her sister mules and the three horses were all neighing as the man tried to hit Minnie and drive her off. Her blanket was twisting around his arms and he couldn't get a good swing at her.

"Hey! Minnie, back off!" Ben approached carefully.

Hearing a familiar voice, Minnie stopped trying to reach the man with her big, square teeth. *It is about time! Get this man away from me!*

Esther took the lantern from Ben and he reached in to grab the furious man by his nearest arm to drag him out of the stall. Minnie took a last kick at him as he was pulled past her hind feet.

"Okay, girl, I've got him. Calm down now!" Ben could not help laughing. "Looks like you picked the wrong mule to steal a blanket from." He yanked the man's arms behind him. "Give me that rope, Esther."

The front door to the stable burst open, and Michael

came in, tucking his shirt tail in. "What is going on? I heard a ruckus out here." He looked at the surly man who Ben was tying to the post, as the door to the stable swung open again to admit all of the boys. They had tumbled out of bed when they heard Michael leaving the house.

"Pa!" Sam's strangled cry made Michael turn to see the little boy, his big blue eyes wide and scared as he grabbed Andy around the waist, and huddled close to him.

"This is your father, son?" Michael beckoned to him and Sam timidly came to let him hold him close. It had taken a long time for him to trust any man, and it took courage now for him to come so close to the man who had savagely beaten him so often. Michael could feel him trembling.

"There is nothing to be scared of. We are all here to take care that he never hurts you again."

"I thought this man was in jail!" Ben glared at the bound man.

"I did too. Right now, we need to get the constable down here. Ben, take one of the horses and see how quick he can get here."

Rose came quietly into the big stable, carrying a bundle of jackets. "Here, all of you are going to catch cold! Come here, Sam." She held out her arms, and he ran to her. "I want all except Andy and Jess to go into the house now. I will be in soon and make you some cocoa. Eli, why don't you go with them? Scoot now!" She turned to Andy and Jess. "While Ben is saddling the mare, you boys go in and dress warmly before you come out to help Michael."

Michael put his arm around his wife, as Esther came in. She had gone back to dress. They watched

Ben swing into the saddle and take off down the drive as Andy and Jess came back from the house.

Rose and Esther moved efficiently around the kitchen, stirring the coals in the range to heat the milk they had poured into a pan for cocoa. Kitty, Katy, Amy and Abby had come down to the kitchen too as they heard the commotion.

"Susey and Meggie are still sleeping." Abby giggled. "Meggie is going to be mad as a hornet when she hears about all of the excitement she missed!" They all settled around the long table, and their chatter made Rose smile in spite of her worry about Sam's father finding him. *How did he get out of jail? I am proud of the way the children handle all of the changes we have had. Even Amy seems happy to be here now, and at first I wondered if I had made a mistake keeping all of them.* She shook her head ruefully, remembering how all of her brother's children had reacted when their parents told them they would be staying on with them.

Stevie was delighted from the first. He loved the prospect of having all of these playmates live with him. He had spent so many lonely hours in their New York apartment with servants to watch over him. Katy had been shocked that her mother and father had not consulted them, but like Stevie, she liked the idea of being with this big, happy family instead of back in the city while her parents were overseas. Amy, on the other hand, could not forgive them for doing this to her. How was she supposed to survive in this little village while they were having a wonderful time in Europe? She had sulked for two days after she heard the news. Gradually, as the family prepared for Thanksgiving, and she met Sarah and Jack, she began to think it would not be so bad…. Especially after Jack let her know he thought she was pretty. Now, just two weeks away from Christmas, she loved her life here.

Esther glanced at the clock. "Good Lord! Three o'clock! It will be time to get up before we get back to bed." She stirred the cocoa into the heated milk and started to pour steaming liquid into the children's cups.

"I think I hear Ben coming back." Rose peered out the window. "Yes, and here comes the constable in his wagon."

Michael and the two boys met them at the door of the stable. They had replaced Minnie's blanket over her back. "Here is a treat for you, girl. You did good!" Michael patted her affectionately, as he gave her one of the apples he kept in a barrel. Smiling, he gave one to each of the other mules and horses. "You all did good!"

"How did you find us? I thought you were in jail over in Utica, waiting for your sentence." He looked at the glowering face of Rusty Murphy with curiosity.

"None of your dang business." The furious man snarled. "Say, if you have food for those dumb animals, how about some for me?"

"Pa, I will bet he is the one who has been taking all the food we have been missing." Andy glowered at the irate man. "I wouldn't give him a crumb."

Ben and the constable, along with a deputy who had recently been added to his police department, came into the lighted stable, and the constable laughed when he saw how the prisoner was trussed up.

"I have to apologize to you, Michael. I got notice this afternoon that this man escaped from prison two weeks ago – right after he got sentenced to life in jail. The man he beat in Utica died as a result of his injuries. I am sorry about this and glad you took care of it so well." He glared at the sullen man. "How did you know where to come? How did you know where Sam was? And why would you want to find him? You must have heard that he was being well taken care of."

"Yeah – I heard that. I figured if they wanted to keep the little brat, they could pay me for him. There's so dang many kids wandering around here that I never got a chance to get him alone to make him get me some money. I would have starved if they didn't have those buildings where they keep their food."

"Where have you been sleeping?" Andy was puzzled. "How come none of us has seen you?"

"I think I know the answer to that now." Ben scratched his head and grinned ruefully. "I should have paid more attention to Eli. He has been telling me that he heard noises out here almost every night for quite some time. I will bet he has been sleeping in the loft back there." He pointed to the back of the stable where spare parts and furniture were stored overhead."

The sullen look on the man's face let them know that Ben had guessed right.

Chapter FIFTEEN

A Baker's Dozen

The day before Christmas a big parcel was delivered by the Railroad Station's delivery cart. Inside were beautifully wrapped presents for everyone at the farm from Rose's brother and his wife. It bore the return address of Steve's business headquarters in New York.

The family had spent a busy two weeks since Sam's father had been returned to prison, and the farm was able to settle down to the serious business of preparing for Christmas. Rome had become a Christmas shopping paradise. The stores along the busy streets were gaily decorated, and the village lamp lighter had wrapped each pole with tinsel that glittered in the coal-gas lights' glow as he lit their coal oil flame each night. The rumor was that next year there would be gas piped into Rome for businesses and homes. Markets displayed fruits and vegetables piled high, and there was a holiday feeling in the village.

Rose and the children visited the shops in small groups. Each one of the children, except for Susey, had given Rose a list of things they wanted to get for the rest of the family, and she helped them to find them. There was an air of excitement and suspense as each of them found a time to wrap their gifts and hide them from each other. Michael and Ben had spent hours in the barn making sleds for everyone to use on the slopes around the farm, and they hinted that they had a great surprise that might be added in time for Christmas.

The company parlor had a huge Scotch Pine tree, cut from their own property, decorated by everyone during a gay party the week before. Garlands of princess pine swung from doorways, and decorated the mantels of the fireplace in each room. The odor of pine greeted visitors at the door, and was made even better as the smell of daily baking for the holidays was added in the kitchen.

Esther, Ben and Eli were there early Christmas morning to join the rest of the family around the pile of presents that had been added beneath the tree.

"What would you like to open first?" Michael grinned, as he watched every pair of eyes focus on the packages that Jane and Steve had sent. "All right! Wait until you all have your package and open them then!" He quickly handed the gaily wrapped packages around, and he and Rose watched as the children eagerly ripped them open. Susey toddled around with her big package until at last she settled down near Rose to open hers.

"Oh! A new winter coat and hat!" Abby was first to lift hers out of her package. It was dark green, with a fur collar. The matching bonnet set off her red curls perfectly. Every package held a winter outfit in beautiful colors that had been chosen to delight its owner.

"Let us really look at you!" Rose clasped her hands as she finished buttoning Susey's blue coat. Andy and Jess were the tallest, and in their navy blue top coats and caps they looked almost grown-up. Joey, Sam, Jamie, Stevie and Eli wore jackets and caps of different bright plaids, chosen from Scotland's most beautiful fabrics.

The six girls had colors that best suited their coloring....
green for Abby, red for Katy, bright blue for Kitty,
pale blue for Amy, yellow for Meggie. They stood
before their family with wide smiles on every face.
"Did you ever see a more beautiful family in your
life!" Rose had tears of happiness in her green eyes.

Michael grinned."What do you think Uncle Andrew
would say if he saw this group?"

Ben shook his head, with a wide smile. "Probably
he would tell you that you need to add some more
room, just in case you grow again!"

Presents were exchanged, and a huge breakfast
consumed before Ben and Michael came in with their
promised surprise. They had crafted ice skates for
every one in the family out in the blacksmith shop.

"Let's skate!" The pond in the back pasture was
frozen over and they lost no time in making a trip
there. Rose and Esther bent to fasten their own skates
as they watched the children move onto the ice. Rose
found herself counting them to make sure they were
all there.

She laughed. "I know what Uncle Andrew would
say if he was here! He would say we have one fine
Baker's Dozen ....Twelve and one to spare!"

A Baker's Dozen